I0654843

J. C. Jehanghier

Life of Cowasjee Jehangir Readymoney

J. C. Jehanghier

Life of Cowasjee Jehangir Readymoney

ISBN/EAN: 9783337847609

Printed in Europe, USA, Canada, Australia, Japan

Cover: Foto ©Raphael Reischuk / pixelio.de

More available books at **www.hansebooks.com**

LIFE OF

SIR COWASJEE JEHANGHIER READYMONEY,

KT., C.S.I., &C., &C.

PREPARED BY

J. COWASJEE JEHANGHIER.

WITH PORTRAIT AND ILLUSTRATIONS.

1890

LIST OF PLATES.

PREFACE.

Y reason for preparing this account of the career and benevolent acts of my dear and revered father is, in addition to a feeling of filial duty and affection, the wish to preserve the memory of his good deeds among those who have benefited by them. The generation which derived direct advantage from them is passing or has passed away; and in the press of new interests and considerations it seemed possible that the claims of Sir Cowasjee Jehanghier to grateful remembrance might be forced out of sight, although his gifts were of a nature to permanently benefit the community, seeing that he dispersed in public charity the large sum of fifteen lakhs, and in private about three more. This record of his life, if it serves no other purpose, should at least preserve his memory among the citizens of Bombay and all Sir Cowasjee's many friends and admirers.

It has been a task of love to peruse the somewhat meagre materials preserved relating to his many public donations, and to extract from them as much matter as seemed likely to be of general interest, and as would give a fair idea of the character and career of Sir Cowasjee Jehanghier. If I have succeeded in compiling a narrative that will be satisfactory to his few remaining contemporaries and interesting to the younger generation, my main object will have been attained. I may at least indulge the hope that among the great Parsee families of Bombay, and among the representatives of Sir Cowasjee's numerous friends, this biography of one of the best known and most distinguished men of his time will be allowed an honoured place in the libraries, and that its shortcomings will be pardoned for the sake of its subject.

JEHANGHIER COWASJEE JEHANGHIER.

London, 5th March, 1890.

LIFE OF

Sir Cowasjee Jehanghier Readymoney,

KT., C.S.I., &c., &c.

WHEN a man has fairly earned, by the admission of his contemporaries, the title of "a Peabody of the East," as the late Sir Cowasjee Jehanghier Readymoney, Kt., C.S.I., did, any apology for telling the story of his life would be unnecessary. There are implied in the sobriquet of "a Peabody" a large-minded benevolence, a sympathy with human suffering, and a sensitive appreciation of the wants of others that may fairly be styled exemplary and that must excite general admiration. Those who were acquainted with Sir Cowasjee Jehanghier Readymoney will know that he possessed all the attributes which one expects to find in the most princely of philanthropists, but the generation which knew of his worth and work is passing away, and it will serve a useful purpose to place on record the details of an eventful life which may well stand as a model for emulation among his own people as well as with all those who seek to make their crown of good deeds. The Parsees have been made famous among prosperous and well-ordered communities by the acts of individuals among whom Sir Cowasjee Jehanghier is entitled to a foremost place, and they cannot but feel gratification at general interest being evinced by the British reader in the career of one of their most prominent representatives.

More than 200 years have elapsed since the Parsees first associated themselves in matters of trade with the English in Western India, and it is useful to recall the fact that the intercourse has been of considerable length and ever-increasing confidence and esteem. Before the English left Surat for Bombay, the Parsees had established a closer business connexion with the factory of the East India Company than with any other European guild, and the Settia (noble or chief) families in particular were famed as being the brokers and intermediaries between the English and the native merchants and producers. Even at this early period, when the Portuguese were at a high point of power and prosperity, the Parsees, either by some happy instinct suggesting to them that the British were the coming race, or because they appreciated their business qualities, associated themselves in a marked manner with the English, and when the head factory was removed from Surat to Bombay the Parsees showed the way in the steady migration of trade that took place to the future capital of Western India. Events have confirmed the wisdom of their choice as well as their foresight. Surat is now neglected by the trader, while Bombay has become one of the most flourishing commercial centres of the whole world. The Parsees have benefited by the great development which has taken place in the trade of Western India, and they can also claim to have contributed much towards creating the existing standard of prosperity. But they have never allowed the main fact to escape from their mind that they are naturally and by old association the colleagues and friends of the English merchants, and the humble and constant supporters of their Government.

What is true of the Parsees as a community is especially true of the ancestors of Sir Cowasjee Jehanghier. The history of the Readymoney family is typical of the fortunes of the Parsee race, and of the development of Bombay. The biographical details of Sir Cowasjee's career will be found both instructive in themselves and stimulating as an example.

The original cause of Sir Cowasjee's family adopting the pseudonym of Readymoney seems to have been the promptitude of their payments. On several pecuniary emergencies they came to the aid of the East India Company, and the tradition is still preserved that on one critical occasion, probably during the Mahratta wars, they sent into the Company's coffers several cartloads of silver. Whatever the origin of the name, there can be no question of the scrupulous integrity with which its inheritors have endeavoured to deserve it and to sustain the lustre of what the late Sir Bartle Frere characterised as a truly English cognomen.

,It was in the early part of the eighteenth century that Sir Cowasjee's ancestors removed to Bombay from Nowsaree, near Surat in Guzrat. Three brothers named Mancherjee Jivanjee, Heerjee Jivanjee, and Temuljee Jivanjee are specially mentioned as having taken up their residence at Bombay in or about 1717. All the brothers carried on a lucrative business, and it is said that Heerjee was the first Parsee merchant to make a voyage to China, with which country they established trade relations. Heerjee's brother Mancherjee followed in his footsteps and went to look after the China firm, and by this means much profit was acquired and the fortunes of the family were established on a sure basis. The Parsees were under great and durable obligations to Heerjee and Mancherjee Readymoney for acting as pioneers of the China trade, from which, as a community, they have derived so much profit. The names of at least two of the ships in which this trade was carried on are pre-served. They were the "Hornby" and the "Royal Charlotte." With the wealth obtained from this source, Heerjee Readymoney bought an extensive estate in Bombay, and took rank among the foremost merchants of his time and country.

Heerjee Readymoney left no male issue. His family consisted of two daughters, the eldest of whom married a member of the well-known Banajee family. Heerjee Readymoney adopted her eldest son, Jehanghier, and made him his heir. Jehanghier Readymoney married Meherbai, the daughter of Heerjee Readymoney's second daughter, and it was for this reason that Heerjee Readymoney made Jehanghier his heir, as his family was re-united in the persons of his grandchildren. Meherbai was on the paternal side a granddaughter of the well-known Ardasir Dady Sett, who was one of the most famous members of the Parsee community, and who was honourably known as the first native of India to establish direct trade between Bombay and England. Dady Nusserwanjee, the founder of the Dady Sett family, came to Bombay in the middle of the eighteenth century, and founded numerous charities (Fire Temples, Dharmsalas, etc.), which are still kept up by funds left by him. Sir Cowasjee Jehanghier was the second son of this marriage—his elder brother Heerjee Readymoney, who is still living, being a successful and energetic merchant.

Sir Cowasjee Jehanghier was born on 24th May—the birthday of Her Most Gracious Majesty the Queen Empress—1812, in the house which had belonged to his maternal grandfather, the great merchant, Dady Sett. This house was known by the latter's name, and was situated in Cowasjee Patell Street in the fort of Bombay. His father Jehanghier resided in the Readymoney mansion in Churchgate Street—an old house which has stood for over a century, and which might be regarded as an Asiatic replica of some of the ancient merchant residences in Venice and Genoa.

The opportunities of education in India were not in those days what they are now. There were really no schools at all worthy of the name, and Sir Cowasjee acquired such knowledge as he possessed of English from the few years he passed at a school kept by Sergeant Sykes in the Fort, where, by the way, he had as a schoolfellow the future second baronet of the Jamsetjee Jeejeebhoy family. In Gujerati, the idiom in use in Western India, and adopted by the Parsees, he was always fluent. There can be no doubt that Sir Cowasjee derived much of his worldly knowledge from his mother, Meherbai, who was a lady of great intelligence and much force of character.

She most carefully trained her son, whom she survived, dying in 1884 at the grand old age of 93. She retained her good health and interest in current events to the end of her life, and will long be remembered in the Parsee community for her tact and benevolence shown especially in the friendly adjudication of family disputes and quarrels. These good points seem to have been the possession of this family. Sir Cowasjee's sister, Dhunbai, was widow of Mr. Framjee Patuck, and a lady of great common-sense; she died in 1882. His second sister married Mr. Dhunjeebhoy Mámá, and died at a comparatively early age, leaving issue one child.

At that period the Parsees were exclusively devoted to commercial pursuits, and the objects of education were confined to carrying on correspondence and keeping accounts. At the early age of fifteen Sir Cowasjee was placed in the office of an English firm, for it was the practice of the Parsees to make their children serve their apprenticeship in an English office under European supervision. In accordance with this custom Sir Cowasjee entered the employment of Messrs. Duncan Gibb and Co., as go-down keeper or clerk in their warehouse. Having acquired considerable experience and business aptitude in this post he transferred his services to the firm of Messrs. Cardwell, Parsons and Co., and after some years spent in their office, to Messrs. Grey and Co. In this way he acquired a thorough knowledge of the trade of Bombay in all its branches. The probationary period of his commercial career lasted from his fifteenth to his twenty-fifth year, and in 1837 he was appointed guaranteed broker to two European firms.

The trade of Bombay passed through a crisis after the withdrawal of the monopoly of the China trade from the East India Company, and as Sir Cowasjee was a keen observer of the signs of the times, the experience and proficiency he acquired in business during those years served him in good stead when the English and native merchants of Bombay turned their energy and attention in the direction of obtaining a larger share in the opium traffic with China. No section of the Bombay community threw itself with more ardour and keenness into the China trade than the Parsees, and none derived greater benefit from it than they did. It is not saying too much to assert that the wealth which they subsequently amassed from trade in this and many other directions had its origin in the promptitude with which they realised the commercial importance of the opening of China that began with the War of 1840 and the Treaty of Nankin.

It so happened that at the very moment when this opportunity presented itself the Parsees were the principal shipowners and shipbuilders of Bombay, and they were therefore able to turn it to the best possible account. For twenty years they retained in their hands what was practically a monopoly of the China trade so far as Western India was concerned, but the introduction of steam raised such formidable competitors in England that they were unable to hold their own with them for want of the necessary appliances and capital. There is no room to hold the opinion, as some have done, that the Parsees evinced a lack of energy and enterprise when the chief ports of China were thrown open to foreign trade by the Treaty of Nankin. As long as ships were made of wood and to carry sails, Bombay was among the most active and prosperous shipyards out of England, but after steam came into vogue its prosperity waned. The Parsees suffered most from this change, but abundant evidence of their sustained energy was supplied when twenty years after the first China War they took the lead in establishing the cotton industry of Bombay, the opportunity for which was afforded by the Civil War in America, and upon which now mainly rests the prosperity of the Presidency of Western India.

It would be somewhat difficult, even if it were desirable, to give a connected narrative of the career of Sir Cowasjee Jehanghier as a merchant. He seems to have commenced on his own account as an independent merchant about the year 1846, and during the next twenty-five years his business transactions were equally extensive and fortunate. Even during the Share mania and panic, which reduced so many wealthy merchants of Bombay to distress, he suffered no material loss, beyond the payment of a considerable sum as one of the promoters of the unfortunate Back Bay Reclamation Scheme. His career in the pursuit of wealth was correctly described as one of uninterrupted prosperity, and it was another of his honourable characteristics that all his dealings were marked by honesty and uprightness. It is not surprising, therefore, that he should have gained the esteem and confidence of all who were brought into business relations with him. He was in every respect qualified by nature to be a successful man of business, and his shrewd sagacity and rare talents enabled him to triumph over his educational defects and to distance most of his competitors in the race for fortune.

The suavity of his manners and address, as well as the regularity of his attendance to all the duties of his position, marked him out at an early period of his life as one who would be called upon to discharge those civic functions which are an essential part of modern civilised life. Not long after his appearance as a merchant on his own account in 1846, he was appointed a Justice of the Peace. He was next nominated a Member of the Board of Conservancy, and in 1860 he was appointed to the still more onerous and responsible position of Commissioner of Income Tax in a city where such a tax was an innovation. The capacity which he displayed in the discharge of all these duties was not less remarkable than that he evinced in the conduct of his own affairs, but it was naturally as Income Tax Commissioner that he obtained the best opportunity of showing how to combine knowledge and tact by carrying out a delicate operation to the equal satisfaction of the Government he served and his own fellow-citizens.

The following gratifying testimony to his services was borne by the late Mr. James Gibbs. President of the Income Tax Commission, and a highly able and much-respected member of the Bombay Council. It was rendered in the course of a public speech, during which Mr. Gibbs' said :—

"I believe that, with the exception of yourself, Sir Cowasjee, I am now the only remaining member of the first Commission which had the working of the tax in this Presidency. I had the honour to preside over that Com-

mission, and I can safely say that for its success the
Commission was mainly indebted to those gentlemen who
were associated with the Government officers in its management, and particularly to you, Sir Cowasjee Jehanghier.
You brought to that Commission tact, firmness, and inde-
pendence of character, which were of very great value;
but, in addition to these, you brought an intimate acquain-
tance with the mercantile community of the city, which
was of the greatest importance in enabling us to assess
the tax. It was mainly owing to this very excellent
information, placed by you at the service of the Commission, that we were able to carry it out so successfully."

It was intended that Sir Cowasjee's services in this
respect should be rewarded with a seat on the Legislative
Council, but before the honour could be conferred upon
him, he was struck down by the grave malady which
confined him to the house for the remainder of his life,
and effectually prevented his taking part in public affairs,
although he did not allow it to interfere with his control
of his own business or the dispensation of his philanthropy.

TOWN MANSION,
OVER A CENTURY OLD.
CHURCHGATE ST. FORT, BOMBAY.

In May, 1871, he received the Companionship of the Order of the Star of India, and in June, 1872, he was created a Knight of the United Kingdom. Both these dignities were universally recognised as being well deserved, and constituted an appropriate recognition of the services which this worthy Parsee merchant had rendered to humanity at large, as well as to his own fellow-citizens.

The Bombay community was not slow to recognise that in honouring him an honour had been conferred by the Sovereign on them all, and an address of congratulation signed by 2.000 citizens. including the Lord Bishop the members of the Governing Council, the Judges, etc., etc., was presented to Sir Cowasjee while confined to his room in his family house at Churchgate Street, by the most prominent representatives of the European and native inhabitants. This deputation waited upon him in October, 1872, and at the same time presented a formal request to Sir Cowasjee to allow a statue to be prepared of him, for which purpose a public subscription of about 25,000 rupees had already been raised. It will be appropriate to quote some of the speeches made on this occasion.

Mr. John Connon, the Chief Magistrate, said :—

"The honourable gentlemen here present I think do themselves honour in being so present assisting at this ceremony, making, as it were, a consensus of opinion, native and European, to do honour to a man who has spread out his hands to help all classes of men, whether they were worshippers of the rising or the setting sun or not. His sun at all events has been goodness, truth, courage, and integrity above everything; and these make a noble sun to honour."

Sir Cowasjee in his reply thus expressed himself :—

"Let me assure you that in my feeble efforts to assist the poor I have only imitated the good works of my forefathers — an example of which was honourably acknowledged by a former Governor of this Presidency more than a century ago. I pray that this feeling may continue among those who will inherit my name, and that so long as the name of Readymoney may exist it shall always be found associated with loyalty and philanthropy. I trust that my statue when erected will induce many of

my countrymen, of all classes and creeds, to remember
that there is more real pleasure in giving than receiving,
and that it is our duty to bestow on others a portion of
the good gifts with which we have been blessed by
God's mercy."

Besides the address presented by his fellow-citizens
of Bombay, several addresses were presented to Sir
Cowasjee by numerous deputations on behalf of associations
and charitable institutions, and representing the inhabitants
of other towns throughout India.

Before proceeding further it may be stated that the
statue was entrusted to the sympathetic hand of Mr.
Woolner, and that as the result of his labours, an expres-
sive and noble figure long ornamented the University Hall
of Bombay. It was removed by his son Mr. Jehanghier
to a more conspicuous position at the entrance of the
University Hall which bore his name, as it was believed
that the Bombay public would thus get a better view of
their benefactor.

Mr. Woolner's heroic (sized) statue of Sir Cowasjee

Jehanghier Readymoney, the distinguished Parsee of Bombay, represents — according to *The Athenæum* — the subject standing erect with his hands interlocked before him; the fingers, so to say, locked together; the arms extended downwards. The attitude is distinctly upright, without effort or the self-assertion which is the vice of modern sculptural design when it is not utterly tame and trivial. The feet are planted well on the ground and in a graceful way a little apart; the head is held erect, and the eyes look straightforwards, and if at all otherwise a little downwards, just as tall men are apt to look. The figure wears full robes and the Parsee hat. The face is said to be a capital likeness, and is certainly remarkable for fine modelling and a general vivacity of expression. The draperies have been most carefully studied and are beautifully composed. The whole looks like what it is—a simply designed, but noble and graceful, work of high art, the complete execution of which is in keeping with the spontaneity of its conception.

In the same connexion it may be noted, in the way of public honour, that when His Royal Highness the

SIR COWASJEE JEHANGHIER, Kt. C.S.I.,
MARBLE STATUE, BY WOOLNER, ESQ. R.A.

Prince of Wales visited Bombay, he honoured Sir Cowasjee by presenting him with a silver medal, a book, and a portrait of himself and of his amiable Princess.

The history of one of the most noteworthy of all Sir Cowasjee's donations is told in the following correspondence, relating to his gift of £200 as a thank-offering for the recovery of His Royal Highness the Prince of Wales from the illness which so nearly proved fatal. The correspondence appeared in the *Times* of 26th January, 1872, and was sent to that paper by Mr. Hugh Owen, secretary of the London Fever Hospital. The present Sir George, then Dr. Birdwood, wrote on 24th January as follows to Mr. Owen :—

"I have the honour to hand over to you the enclosed order on the Bank of England for £200 sterling from Mr. Cowasjee Jehanghier Readymoney, C.S.I., the well-known Parsee merchant of Bombay. In his letter of 14th December to me he says :— 'This gift I make as a free-will offering in token of my heartfelt joy at the recovery of the Prince of Wales from his severe and distressing illness.' Mr. Readymoney's direction to me was, 'in conjunction with a member of the India Council to devote the amount among the most deserving institutions in London for the amelioration of the poor.' I therefore went to Sir Bartle Frere, the late Governor of Bombay, and begged him to refer to His Royal Highness the Prince of Wales as to the institutions among which His Royal Highness might wish the money to be divided. In reply, the private secretary writes :— ' His Royal Highness finds himself placed in a position of some delicacy. London abounds in so many excellent charities that he thinks it would be an invidious and a most difficult task for him to make a selection. If, however, he might be allowed to make a selection, he would propose that a portion of the sum in question should be forwarded to the London Fever Hospital, in consideration of the illness from which, by the mercy of God and the skill of his physicians, His Royal Highness has just happily recovered.' . . . . The suggestion is so good that I have made the whole amount of the order payable to your treasurer. It were a pity to divide it. Sir Bartle approves of my determination, and I know that Mr. Ready-money will with all his heart and mind."

On this act *Punch* printed the following amusing commentary:—"No mistake in the name. As 'a thanks-offering from India,' a contemporary announces that, on account of the recovery of the Prince of Wales, a charitable donation of £200 has been sent to London by Mr. Cowasjee Jehanghier Readymoney. Anybody would have given Mr. Readymoney credit for having earned his name, and now everybody must see that he well deserves it. Is Mr. Readymoney a Parsee? At any rate he is the reverse of Parsi-monious."

Sir Cowasjee Jehanghier did not become famous, nor will he be remembered on account of the dignity with which he discharged his civic duties, and it was not by taking an active part in the administration of public affairs that he gained the high esteem in which he was held by his contemporaries, who knew and admired the character of the man. The harsh decree which confined him to the house from a tedious and painful malady during the last fourteen years of his life, prevented his playing that part in civic and legislative circles for which his experience and position alike suited him. His work as a Justice of the Peace, as a Conservator, and as a Commissioner of Income Tax, showed what he might have done, had not considerations of health intervened and put a peremptory end to his public occupations. We have now to consider that more magnanimous character of a philanthropist in which he gained a world-wide reputation, that affords the principal motive for the preparation of this biography and its ample justification.

It was as a philanthropist that Sir Cowasjee Jehanghier became famous, and it is now time to specify and place on permanent record the objects of his philanthropy, and to describe the course of a charity which was thoroughly catholic in its dispensation.

Charity was an inherited virtue in the family of Readymoney. Sorabjee Readymoney in 1790 fed 2,000 people daily during a great famine which fell upon Bombay in that year. It was a noteworthy feature of his charity that no discrimination was to be made between race and religion among those succoured. Sorabjee was also the patron of many Bombay charities, and he specially distinguished himself by his aid to his suffering kinsmen in Gujarat. In 1805 Ardasir Dady, Sir Cowasjee's maternal grandfather, distinguished himself in a like manner by feeding 5,000 people for three weeks during a similar visitation. It will thus be seen that both on the maternal and the paternal side Sir Cowasjee inherited instincts of charity and an example of benevolence.

The first charitable work with which Sir Cowasjee's name was publicly associated on a large scale was the Hospital at Surat. In a letter, dated 26th February, 1857, to the Bombay Government, Sir Cowasjee stated that during a recent visit he had been struck by the want of a Hospital at Surat, which had been the early seat of both the Parsees and the East India Company. He offered to contribute towards the construction of a suitable building the sum of 30,000 rupees. The correspondence relating to this project went on for a period of three years, and in the end Sir Cowasjee contributed not less than 66,000 rupees towards the realisation of his design. The delay had proved very tedious, and the following characteristic letter from Sir Cowasjee shows how quite unnecessary it was. The letter was dated Bombay, 26th May, 1860, and addressed to Mr. A. F. Bellasis :—

"DEAR SIR,—I am gratified to receive your kind note with the copy of your letter to Government on the Hospital. I am very much indebted to you for the interest you took in it. All the delay that occurred I attribute to the Department of Chief Engineer, who is a very lazy man and neglectful. Last year he never even remembered to open the second designs sent in by gentlemen, on his invitation by public advertisement, for weeks after the proper advertised time to open, and when opened he did not bring the result with expedition as any business man would have done. To prevent any delay I left everything to Government, which you will observe from my correspondence.

"Even when, by the reckless manner of advertisement inviting tenders for designs, re-advertising when none accepted, he must have incurred expenses at least nearly, if not fully, equal to the amount of prize, I never interfered, fearing he might think I was obstructing him."

His final letter to the Government of Bombay, completing the payment for the Hospital building, is also interesting. It is dated 20th January, 1863 :—

"SIR,—I had the honour to receive your letter, dated this day, just now, and have the pleasure to enclose you a cheque on the Bombay Bank for 21,042 rupees (twenty-one thousand and forty-two) the full sum of extras, 11,955 rupees and 1,436 rupees for clock tower, and 7,652 rupees for fence walling, gate, and approaches, etc.

"Please convey my best thanks to the Governor in Council for their offer of paying the moiety of excess, 5,977 rupees, which I consider a most liberal offer on the part of the Government; but as I wished from the outset the building should be at my expense, I therefore beg most respectfully to decline their offer to pay the moiety of excess.

"I beg most respectfully that the Government will

thoroughly examine all accounts, etc., etc., and to see that the expenditure has been carefully superintended, and an order should be sent immediately to carry on the works for outhouses, railing, and finishing the Hospital vigorously. Accept my best thanks for your kindness in bringing the subject to a speedy termination."

The Hospital was formally opened by the late Sir Bartle Frere, then Governor of Bombay, but Sir Cowasjee's health did not admit of his being present. The event went off with great *éclat*, and Sir Cowasjee received con-gratulations from all sides. The Secretary of State, in a despatch written in April, 1863, conveyed his special thanks for his "munificent liberality."

The correspondence relating to the Surat Hospital had not closed when Sir Cowasjee made a second noble offer to alleviate suffering humanity. This was to provide at his own expense an Eye Hospital for Bombay. Sir Charles Wood, then Secretary of State, wrote the following despatch on this offer :—

SIR COWASJEE JEHANGHIER OPHTHALMIC HOSPITAL.
BYCULLAH. BOMBAY.

"THE INDIA OFFICE, LONDON,

"*25th June*, 1863.

"HIS EXCELLENCY THE GOVERNOR IN COUNCIL, BOMBAY.

"SIR,—I have considered in Council your letters, dated 28th March and 13th April, 1863, relating to the munificent offer of Mr. Cowasjee Jehanghier to contribute 50,000 rupees towards the construction of an Eye Hospital on the premises of the Grant Medical College.

"I do not doubt that the construction of a building especially adapted for the treatment of diseases of the eye will be found highly beneficial, and I have to request that Mr. Cowasjee Jehanghier may be informed of the high sense I entertain of his liberality in contributing so largely towards the provision of such a building."

It will be observed that Sir Cowasjee's offer was one of 50,000 rupees, but the total cost of erecting the building proved to be 97,143 rupees, all of which he defrayed. The Governor-General in Council sent their acknowledgments to the ·'philanthropic donor," and Sir Charles Wood wrote from London to express "the sincere thanks of Her

Majesty's Government to Mr. Cowasjee Jehanghier."
Finally, at a meeting of the Government of Bombay in
Council, the following resolution was passed:—

"His Excellency the Governor in Council congratu-
lates Mr. Cowasjee Jehanghier on the completion of this
building, which will prove a lasting memorial of his
philanthropy."

The Civil Engineering College at Poonah was another
monument of his generosity. His principal motive in contributing 50,000 rupees towards this Institution was to
provide his fellow-countrymen with the means of taking up
and pursuing another learned profession, and full credit for that
motive is given in the tablet of inscription placed within the
building. The speech made, on the occasion of his opening
the College in 1865, by the late Sir Bartle Frere, who had
always appreciated the work of Sir Cowasjee Jehanghier,
affords ample evidence of what that sympathetic and broad-
minded statesman thought of the philanthropic acts of the
Parsee benefactor. Sir Bartle Frere spoke as follows:—

SIR COWASJEE JEHANGHIER CIVIL HOSPITAL, SURAT.

SIR COWASJEE JEHANGHIER COLLEGE OF SCIENCE,
POONAH.

"We have in the first place to perform this day a duty of justice and gratitude in acknowledging the noble benefactions of Mr. Cowasjee Jehanghier Readymoney, to whom we owe it that this building when completed may be something better than a commodious shed. I greatly regret that the state of his health prevents Mr. Cowasjee from being here present to-day to receive in person an acknowledgment for his liberality. But his absence has at least one advantage, that it permits me to speak more unreservedly than I should otherwise have ventured to do of our obligations to him, and to refer to one or two circumstances connected with his gift which are so characteristic of him that I cannot forbear to call them to your recollection. Thus it will, I know, interest many here present to be reminded that his offer of £5,000 towards building this College was coupled with the gift of a similar sum to aid the Strangers' Friend Society in building a home in Bombay for destitute Europeans. This, as you know, is not by any means a solitary instance of his liberality, and the gift was marked by other traits no less characteristic of the practical business-like habits without which such liberality must too often fail to secure its object. The large sums he contributed were paid into the Treasury as soon as he was aware that his benefaction had been accepted. On this as on all other occasions Mr. Cowasjee Jehanghier was anxious to justify the thoroughly English surname which he had chosen for himself, and acted in accordance with what was the old boast 'of the great native merchants of Bombay, and will, I trust, ever continue to be the practice of all that deserve to be numbered among that honourable body —that their word was as good as their bond. . . . I feel assured, that in enlisting in upon to his countrymen a new liberal and independent profession, Mr. Cowasjee Jehanghier has not only done well for his own fame and conferred a lasting benefit upon his own people, but that he has also added his contribution to the strength and stability of our empire in India."

The Strangers' Home referred to in Sir Bartle Frere's speech had been suggested by Sir Cowasjee and sanctioned by the Government at the same time as the Poonah

Engineering College. On 7th March, 1863, Sir Cowasjee deposited with Government the 50,000 rupees he had promised. Great remissness was shown in carrying out the project, and on 22nd March, 1871, more than seven years afterwards. Sir Cowasjee wrote the Secretary to Government the following angry letter:—'

"Sir,—Since 1863, when I paid Messrs. Ritchie, Stewart, and Co., for building a Home for European Strangers, 50,000 rupees on certain conditions, which building business was afterwards transferred to Government, and up to now no such house is built, I consider all the correspondence on the subject is at an end, and I demand instant return of my money with interest. I consider Government has treated very badly not only me but also the poor destitute Europeans. My increased illness suggests that I should do some other charity with the said money."

The matter was not finally settled until the early part of 1873, when certain categorical propositions put forward by Sir Cowasjee as the conditions on which he would allow his donation in 1863 of 50,000 rupees, with accumulated interest, to remain for the benefit of the Strangers' Fund, were accepted by the Government. The principal of these were that the Fund be called the Sir Cowasjee Jehanghier Fund for the relief of poor suffering Europeans, that Government should take charge of the Fund and allow 6 per cent. on it, and that a suitable Home for the European Strangers' Friend Society should be provided by Government with as little delay as possible.

The correspondence relating to this long pending transaction was necessarily voluminous, and expression is given in many of his letters to Sir Cowasjee's disappointment at the manner in which the matter had been allowed to hang fire. Sir Cowasjee felt more than anything else that he might personally be held to share in the blame for the delay. Space may therefore be made for the following letter, dated January, 1873, to his valued friend, Sir George Birdwood.

"MY DEAR BIRDWOOD,—From the above you will

observe instead of 50,000 rupees, my agreement which was delayed fulfilling by Bombay Government up to now, I give up interest also, and that is an additional gift on my part of 22,000 rupees which I am not bound to pay, as note was deposited only for security for fulfilment of my agreement on distinct understanding interest to be returned to me when building commenced to build, which is not built yet. In the meantime, I suffered by the report spread by my enemies that I broke my agreement, in which any sane man will pronounce I was perfectly right. Please take this letter, in justice to myself, to any gentlemen who have such impression that I am not fulfilling my promise, and to clear me from such fault at once, and write me, please, so that I remain satisfied that I left no enemy in this world.

"Yours sincerely, Cowasjee Jehanghier."

It is now time to describe the most important of all his benefactions, viz.: his gifts of two lakhs (200,000 rupees) to the Elphinstone College and of one lakh for a Hall for the Bombay University. On January 31st, 1863,

Sir Cowasjee addressed the following letter to the Secretary of the Bombay Government.

"SIR,—The want of a suitable College building has been very much felt in Bombay for years past, and the Hon. Mr. Erskine when here exerted himself very much to have one erected, but, for want of the support of the community, the matter remained in abeyance. Last year, when Baboola Tank premises was considered unsuitable, a great difficulty arose how to provide for additional rent for engaging another building—the Tankerville. Through the exertion of Sir A. Grant, the difficulty was temporarily removed by receiving contributions from a few native gentlemen. The lease of the Tankerville expires in about twelve months, after which much higher rent will have to be paid. The day before yesterday I called on Sir A. Grant, Bart., and offered to pay to Government, towards building a new College, 100,000 rupees, provided Government pay the rest, whatever required, to purchase site and complete the building, etc., etc., that are required not only for the present but future wants of the place, and

SIR COWASJEE JEHANGHIER BUILDING OF ELPHINSTONE COLLEGE

which are to be kept in good condition afterwards at the expense of Government, and in case—which God forbid!—the building falls or is destroyed, through whatever cause, the same should be rebuilt at the expense of Government. The building ought to have within its walls or in detached premises a gymnasium, boarding house for mofussil boys, and, in short, whatever is considered necessary by Sir A. Grant. The building to be erected under entire control of Government, which is also to have discretion in selecting site. In case amount on part of Government exceeds a lakh, Government is to pay more, and the present usual rule of half by half should be waived in this undertaking, which is a national one and for general public good, and not confined to the purposes of my or any one religion.

"The above offer I make with my heartfelt and sincere pleasure, seeing the Government is composed of active and energetic members, and that ever to be worshipped its present head, His Excellency the Governor, for his general desire to do public good, and hope, therefore, to see that the new College, if terms are suitable to Government, will be built and ready by May 1st, 1864."

The official reply, dated February 7th, 1863, to this offer may well be given:—

"Sir,—I am directed to acknowledge the receipt of your letter dated 31st January last, offering to contribute the sum of rupees one lakh towards the construction of a suitable building in Bombay, on the following conditions, viz.:—1, That the Government contribute an equal sum; 2, That no other private individual be invited to subscribe; 3, That it be promptly begun and carried out.

"In reply, I am desired to inform you that His Excellency the Governor in Council has much satisfaction in accepting your munificent offer on the conditions prescribed. It will also afford His Excellency in Council much gratification to associate your name with the building.

"With the view of determining the best means of giving effect to the Grant, a committee has been appointed, composed of the gentlemen named in the margin (Sir A. Grant, Bart., E. I. Howard, Esq., G. M. Birdwood, Esq., M.D.); with whom I am desired to request you will associate yourself as a member.

"His Excellency in Council will have great pleasure in bringing to the notice of Her Majesty's Government this further proof of the enlightened interest which you have long evinced in the advancement of education in Bombay.

"I have, etc., H. L. ANDERSON, Chief Secretary."

On February 11th, Sir Cowasjee replied, enclosing his cheque for the lakh of rupees, and at the same time respectfully declining a seat on the Committee, as he had every confidence in the judgment of Government. This noble offer so promptly carried into effect, naturally evoked loud expressions of public and official recognition. The Government of India expressed its high satisfaction at "this fresh instance of Mr. Cowasjee Jehanghier's enlightened liberality."

Sir Bartle Frere wrote on April 30th, 1863, from Mahableshwar, the following letter to the princely donor:—

"MY DEAR SIR,– Sir Alexander Grant has told me of your munificent gift of a lakh of rupees for University

Buildings. I need not tell you how highly pleased I am at this fresh instance of enlightened liberality, and how much gratified I shall feel in reporting it to the Governor-General and to Her Majesty's Principal Secretary of State. I make no doubt but that we shall be able to arrange for meeting your wishes with regard to completing the building at Government expense, without further appeal to private liberality beyond your own magnificent gift. By this I mean such an integral portion of the Buildings which the University will require as shall form in itself a separate monument of your generous desire to contribute to the wants of the University. You are doubtless aware of the almost infinite extension of such wants as time rolls on, and as the duties as well as the needs of the University increase. You would, I am sure, wish to see the example you have so worthily set, followed by a numerous body of University benefactors in this and in many succeeding generations; and you would not, I am sure, wish to debar the University from looking forward to a constant succession of such benefactors, nor to exclude them from following your example by adding to and

SIR COWASJEE JEHANGHIER UNIVERSITY HALL,
BOMBAY.

endowing the edifice which you will have the credit of having been the first to raise.

"Believe me, MY DEAR SIR, very truly yours,

"H. B. E. FRERE."

Sir Cowasjee's reply to this letter should also be read:—

"MY DEAR SIR,—Last week I had the honour to receive your Excellency's letter as to the new building for the Bombay University. I am intensely gratified to see my offer being entertained. This is a further proof of your liberal and energetic Government, for I only addressed to Sir A. Grant on Tuesday, and the same replied from Mahableshwar on the following Thursday, the 30th ult. I owe already a debt of gratitude to your Excellency for personally taking laborious and painstaking interest in bringing arrangements to a close in so short a time for erecting three most magnificent buildings, that were urgently needed for years past for the benefit of the general community, which, if your Excellency will allow me to say so, would in former days have taken five years.

Your Excellency's Government will supply, I am sure, Bombay's wants for fifty years in advance, and will bring all its arrears of fifty years back. May every happiness and blessing attend you and yours."

His liberality, as will be seen, did not stop with the gift of one lakh. A site was selected, the designs of Mr. Trubshawe for a noble building were passed, and work towards its erection commenced—all with remarkable and commendable promptitude and celerity. At this stage a hitch occurred through the cost considerably exceeding the estimate, and again Sir Cowasjee came to the rescue, as is explained in the following letter to Sir Alexander Grant, dated June 23rd, 1864 :—

"MY DEAR SIR ALEXANDER,— It has been brought to my notice that the Committee for carrying out the Elphinstone College Buildings, which are to bear my name, find themselves in difficulties owing to the high prices of labour and materials at present ruling in Bombay. I hear that the design which you selected for the College Buildings, and which was estimated by the Civil Architect to cost only one lakh and eighty thousand rupees, cannot now be executed for less than four lakhs and fifty thousand rupees.

"Under these circumstances, I am willing again to come forward and offer to Government another lakh of rupees, making in all two lakhs, as my contribution to the Elphinstone College Buildings.

"But, in order to prevent all misunderstanding and disappointment for the future, I beg to stipulate that I make this offer on condition that Government will under-take to find all the remainder of the sum for carrying out Mr. Trubshawe's design; secondly, that they will carry out that design intact, except so far as improvements and additions are concerned; thirdly, that the buildings may be *bonâ fide* commenced within six weeks from this date. And if the above conditions be not accepted, or if any of them be violated, I shall beg to retract the offer which I now make.

"Yours sincerely,

"COWASJEE JEHANGHIER."

Sir Bartle Frere, who was then Governor of Bombay, and who had gained the hearts of the people of India by his ready sympathy, hastened to reply to this letter, which he did on the following day:—

"My dear Sir,—I have just heard from Sir Alexander Grant of your noble offer to forward the completion of the Elphinstone College. I will not await the arrival of his official letter before thanking you for such an act of well-judged liberality, which is peculiarly gratifying to me, whether I regard it as Governor of the Presidency, or as the Chancellor of the University. I trust now that I may have the pleasure at no distant period of congratulating you on the completion of the College, and that you may long live to see the younger members of your community trained to learning and sound morals in the building your liberality will have provided.

"Believe me, my dear Sir,

"Very faithfully yours,

"H. B. E. Frere."

At the laying of the foundation-stone of the Elphinstone College buildings on 7th March, 1866, Sir Bartle Frere made the following encomiastic remarks on the subject of Sir Cowasjee's liberality:—

" I need not tell you how much satisfaction it gives me to comply with your request to be present this day, and to lay the corner-stone of this building. It is not on an occasion like this that there is much of novelty in what can be said, but there are some features in the history of this day's proceedings which I should be sorry to let pass without a word of comment; and in particular let me bring to your recollection that the gentleman to whose liberality we owe this building is not the first of his family who has thus distinguished himself. I find that a paternal ancestor of his was one of those to whom Bombay and the Parsees of Bombay are indebted for their share in the great China trade. Heerjee, who is still well remembered among the older inhabitants of Bombay, was the first, in conjunction with the founder of the great house of Forbes and Company, to commence that trade which has enriched so many of his countrymen. It was he who by the promptitude and punctuality of his payments obtained for his descendants the honourable and characteristic name of Readymoney, and I lately found in some unpublished letters of the great Duke of Wellington —not in one letter, but in three or four addressed to the then Governor of Madras and the Governor-General of India—records of his opinion of the firm, and expressions of his belief that that firm had made their mercantile undertakings subservient to the good of the British Government in Western India. I am told, too, that on his maternal side the gentleman to whose liberality we owe this building is descended from one who is still remembered as a leader of the Parsees in his day, and of whom it is told that the Governor of those days, Mr. Jonathan Duncan, ordered the great bell of St. Thomas' Church to be tolled, as a testimony of the public respect to his memory, as his funeral passed by. These things are not insignificant in a community like that of the Parsees."

A subsequent delay chafed Sir Cowasjee's spirit so much that on 22nd May, 1867, he addressed the Governor of Bombay, Sir Vesey Fitzgerald, the following eminently characteristic letter:—

"RIGHT HONOURABLE SIR,—On the 8th August, 1863, I paid rupees one lakh, and the remaining cost to be defrayed by Government, for erecting a building for the Bombay University. The site was chosen opposite Churchgate Street entrance on the Esplanade. I have heard nothing further this last four years. The materials are now greatly cheaper, owing to the late cessation of building mania in Bombay. Allow me to suggest that Government should take immediate action in the matter. Pardon the liberty I take in addressing your Excellency this letter, as Government machinery is so unwieldy that a force of elephants could not move it unless your Excellency takes personal interest, as the subject of this letter is of public importance. The late, my much esteemed, Governor, Sir Bartle Frere, was always willing to hear from me on such subjects, and he always took personal interest in all my public charity which not only helped people, but also helped Government very much, because Government is bound to erect all these public buildings, and I think whatever help I contribute in such undertakings is to be considered a saving from public revenue—the contributors to the latter are poor cultivators of the interior."

Sir Cowasjee was, naturally, most anxious that full effect should be given to the original arrangement, by which his name would be closely associated and identified with the new College buildings, and so, in 1869, we find him approaching the Government on the subject, and quoting what had been said many years before by the Committee entrusted with the execution of the design. Their words were to the following effect:—"The Committee are of opinion that the edifice should be called 'Cowasjee Jehanghier Buildings;' this name will bear nearly the same relation to Elphinstone College as Neville's Buildings does to Trinity College, Cambridge, or the 'Canterbury' and 'Peckwater' quadrangles do to Christ Church, Oxford. The name of Elphinstone College

—a national institution, the first college that was affiliated to the University of Bombay, cannot, of course, be altered." Effect was given to the donor's wishes by the erection of a marble tablet over the centre door, bearing the following inscription :—

"The Cowasjee Jehanghier Buildings, for the use of the Elphinstone College, were erected at a cost of   rupees, of which two lakhs were contributed by Mr. Cowasjee Jehanghier Readymoney, C.S.I. ; completed 18   ."

In March, 1874, Sir Cowasjee voluntarily sent 10,000 rupees for the special purpose of furnishing the Hall, as indicated in the following letter :—

" SIR,—I have the pleasure to enclose you a cheque on Oriental Bank Corporation for 10,000 rupees, to commemorate the auspicious and eventful day of inaugurating the (with His Excellency's permission) Sir Cowasjee Jehanghier Hall for University, by furnishing with furniture, and Government is to pay usual share, or their part, 20,000 rupees, so in all 30,000 rupees, which will enable Government to purchase furniture of first class, and purchase for the same to be ordered through some responsible persons who have knowledge of such things." The Government of Bombay were unable to accept the conditions imposed by the donor, when Sir Cowasjee presented the sum unfettered by any conditions.

Among his minor benefactions may be mentioned his founding of a Lunatic Asylum at Hydrabad, in Scinde. Sir Cowasjee had originally wished to patronise or endow some public work at Kurrachee, but on official representation he decided to found a Lunatic Asylum at Hydrabad. Sir Alexander Grant pointed out to him that as the people of Scinde did not like the climate of Kurrachee it should be constructed at the old capital of the Province. Sir Cowasjee's offer was contained in the following letter, dated 13th February, 1868 :—

" SIR,—Sir A. Grant, Bart., who returned from Scinde the day before yesterday, informed me that he had found great want of a Lunatic Asylum with gardens attached at Hydrabad, in Scinde. I therefore beg to offer 50,000 rupees towards a substantially-built building, and a large garden, if Government will defray the remainder of the cost, whatever it may be, and maintain the same at Government's charge. An assistant surgeon or surgeon of the Government's covenanted service should be its Superintendent, as now at Bombay.

"The offer I now make is with the view of saving so much of the public revenue, and at the same time helping the people of Scinde to provide for their lunatics without asking subscriptions from them. It is also a great satisfaction to me that I conscientiously discharge my duty to Him who has entrusted me with a little of His worldly riches with a command that I should judiciously spend the same wherever need be, towards providing for the helpless, of whatever caste or creed. The asylum must always be in charge of covenanted doctors under Government service, as at present in Colaba Asylum for Bombay Presidency. The building and garden to be kept in repair for ever. The Government will be pleased to send me final answer on 13th May, i.e., within next three months."

After some correspondence, relating more to the amount of Government supervision than to the institution itself, the proposed building was sanctioned and commenced, and Sir Cowasjee handed over his promised contribution of 50,000 rupees. One passage in this letter calls for notice, as showing the quaintness and the practicality of Sir Cowasjee's views and language. He wrote:—"I beg most earnestly the attention of Government for the building to be built of modern style, so as to be attractive to the passers-by, who may inquire, and finding what it contains may go in and drop some money for the additional comforts of their co-creatures, the lunatics, and at the same time, for centuries to come, such style of buildings will give reflection with high honour to the name of Englishmen's architecture."

Minor, but still interesting, objects of his munificence were the fountain in front of the Cathedral, which was erected at a cost of 10,000 rupees from the designs of the late Sir Gilbert Scott; a grant of 8,000 rupees to the Bombay Branch of the Royal Asiatic Society for the purchase of coins and teak presses; and a gift of several thousand rupees for the construction of a clock tower at Kapurwange. In connection with the last named gift, the ever-increasing amount of the estimated cost caused the donor considerable vexation, and drew from him the following exceedingly characteristic letter, dated 18th June, 1867 :—

"MY DEAR SIR,—Your kind letter to hand of 14th inst., and regret much to hear the estimated cost of the clock tower at Kapurwange further increased at once to 350 per cent. from its original estimate after being very carefully made by professional engineers. First it was 1,500 rupees, and then I received final estimate increased to 2,000 rupees. The latter sum I paid at once, and an increase of 25 per cent. is not a little. I must now beg most respectfully to decline to pay any further sum.

"It is the mistake of the Kapurwange people, who, if not legally, are morally bound to complete the tower at their own expense, as all the arrangements up to now have been in their hands and I never interfered. I am a perfect stranger to the place, and only obeyed the commands of Him who entrusted to my care a little of worldly riches that I should always spend for the welfare of His creatures. The inhabitants of Kapurwange alone will derive benefit from it."

It is scarcely surprising that these repeated acts of munificence attracted as much attention at the hands of the Press as of Government. *The Times* wrote as follows on the subject of Sir Cowasjee's benefactions :—

"This Parsee merchant has, with the most large-hearted liberality, spent his fortune in works of public utility and charity, without respect of race or creed, in those whom he has so assisted. His private charities have been many, and the sum of his public benefactions amounts to 1,270,508 rupees."

The opinion of a leading Anglo-Indian Journal, *The Bombay Gazette*, is also well worth recording :—

"His princely donations given for works of public

utility and his contributions for the relief of the suffering and the distressed in all parts of India and Europe, have established his claim to the character of a philanthropist, and it was, perhaps, no violent straining of a metaphor to call him the 'Peabody of the East.' His charity has been almost always singularly discriminating, and if it had occasionally a tendency to arrest attention, yet it was always dispensed without a distinction of colour or creed. His donations to various charities and public institutions in England and on the Continent have made his name familiar to many in the West, while in India his benefactions have long entitled him to the respect and gratitude of all classes of people. For nearly a quarter of a century (1872) his charity has continued to flow in all directions, and he is said to have given in this way nearly fifteen lakhs of rupees."

Among his charitable gifts of a cosmopolitan character none was more calculated to attract attention than his donation of £1,000 to the fund in aid of the wounded during the great Franco-German war. The gift was made in the accompanying letter to Sir Bartle Frere:—

"BOMBAY, 10*th September*, 1870.

"MY DEAR SIR,—I have the pleasure to enclose you a bill for £1,000, costing me 10,726 rupees at 1s. 10¾d., at sight, drawn by Oriental Bank Corporation on Bank of England, and I have endorsed to your good self, which please realise and pay to the Prussian and French authorities on my behalf, £500 to each of them, for distribution among their wounded of the armies presently engaged in several battles in Europe.

"Though the occurrence took place in a foreign land at so great a distance, I could not obtain a peace to my mind ever since the fearful slaughter and maiming of human beings; now from this day I shall satisfy myself that I served people in great distress with little money I can spare to forward for the good of my co-creatures.

"You must pardon the trouble I put you in, but you will forgive me when I say you were my good and honoured late Governor of Bombay. . . . Please inform the Secretary of State for India, officially, of the deed of one of Her Majesty's Indian subjects assisting England's neighbours in their distress.

"I remain, MY DEAR SIR, yours sincerely,

"COWASJEE JEHANGHIER."

In concluding the list of Sir Cowasjee's benefactions, reference may be made to the assistance he rendered the sufferers by a great fire in the Camatepoora district in 1850, when a large number of small houses were destroyed, and their inmates rendered homeless. He went to their

cases of the applicants for relief, and disbursed upwards of 1,200 rupees in rebuilding 40 habitations. In 1852 he gave 3,500 rupees to the funds of the Sir Jamsetjee Jeejeebhoy Parsee Benevolent Institution; 1,000 rupees to the Perry Testimonial Fund; and sums of 600 rupees and more to the Bandora Charitable Dispensary, the Lawrie School of Industry, then under the charge of the late Dr. George Buist, and other institutions. In 1857 he presented 1,000 rupees to the Scottish Orphanage Clothing Fund, and in subsequent years 1,500 rupees to the

Building Fund, and two other sums of 1,000 rupees each for general purposes, besides 540 rupees to distribute sweetmeats to the little children, in remembrance of Sir Joseph Arnould, late a judge of the Supreme and High Courts at Bombay, on the anniversary of his birthday. In 1861, during the famine in the North-West Provinces, he contributed 1,000 rupees to the Relief Fund, but he did a great deal more on this occasion than to make this money gift. Money was immediately required for prompt relief, and pending the collections to be made, he came forward and placed 90,000 rupees, in cash, at the disposal of Government, without security and without interest. He also contributed 5,000 rupees to the Albert Orphanage; 540 rupees for experiments in vaccination; 3,810 rupees to the funds for poor and distressed Persian Zoroastrians; 2,000 rupees to the Lancashire Relief Fund; 1,000 rupees to the Manchester Distress Fund; and 18,920 rupees, in small sums, for relief to sufferers from famine or lack of work. His thoughtfulness extended even to the thirsty wayfarer, for whom he provided drinking fountains throughout Bombay at a cost of 22,000 rupees. Sir Cowasjee seems

SIR COWASJEE JEHANGHIER FOUNTAIN,
REGENT'S PARK, LONDON.

to have regarded drinking fountains as supplying one of the chief wants of humanity—which is not surprising in the inhabitant of an Eastern country—for he gave 13,540 rupees for the erection of the Regent's Park Fountain, which bears his name, and which was opened by Her Royal Highness the Princess Mary of Teck in 1869. He also gave 7,500 rupees for a pillar in Colaba Church, in memory of those who fell in the Afghan War; 5,000 rupees for the St. Zavier's College Tower; 2,500 rupees to the Victoria Museum; 1,100 rupees to the East India Association; 25,000 rupees to the English School Fund of the Nowsaree Madrasa; 5,000 rupees to the Parsee Punchayat Fund for teaching Oriental Languages; 10,000 rupees to the Girls' School, Khetwady, Bombay; 5,400 rupees to the Indian Turf Society for the importation of English blood horses; 5,000 rupees to the Bombay University, in January, 1868, for the founding of a Latin Scholarship, to be awarded each year to the best candidate in Latin at the Matriculation Examination; 2,500 rupees to the St. Zavier's College for a Latin Scholarship; 2,005 rupees for the Duke of Edinburgh Reception Fund in Bombay; and 1,200 rupees for a seal for the Bombay University. In addition to eighteen lakhs of public charities, he contributed certainly not less than four lakhs in private donations. In the lifetime of Sir Cowasjee, he contemplated endowing a fire-temple at Mazagon, but his untimely death prevented him from carrying out his resolve. After Sir Cowasjee's death, in order to give effect to his wish, his son, Mr. Jehanghier, set apart 23,000 rupees for the maintaining of the said fire-temple and called it after Sir Cowasjee.

Although Sir Cowasjee was confined to his room for the last fourteen years of his life by the severe form of rheumatic gout from which he suffered, he never relaxed his supervision of his business affairs. Up to the last hour of his life he took the most lively interest in what was going on around him: He was obliging in his disposition, and condescending in his manner. Before his illness, and even afterwards, he was easily accessible to those who came to seek his advice or his assistance, and rarely did they go away unsatisfied or disappointed. The bounty of his charity did not prevent his exercising his powers of discrimination, and he always reserved to himself the right of determining the particular direction in which he should bestow his benefactions. If his charity was ever criticised it was on the ground of being capricious, but the only foundation for the charge was, that he was not influenced by purely local considerations, and that his breadth of view compelled him to limit his dispensations only by humanity itself. As a matter of fact no man had fewer enemies, or was more universally admired, and if he had not been stricken down with his painful malady in the prime of his life, there is no saying what further honours and fame would not have fallen to his share. When the end came in July, 1878, he was only 67 years of age, but considering that he had been confined to his room more than fourteen years, his age was greater than the mere number of his years.

It was only when they lost him that the Bombay community seemed to realise the extent of his services, and the magnitude of its loss. Obituary notices of "the Peabody of the East" appeared in all the leading papers. A special notice from the Government of Bombay was

inserted in the official *Gazette* to the following effect:—
"By his death the Government has lost one of its most loyal subjects, India a most generous benefactor, and the town and island of Bombay one of its most upright and independent citizens." At the University the following reference to the loss suffered by that institution in the death of this "venerable philanthropist" was made by Professor Peterson:—"You will not, I am sure, think it out of place, if, before beginning my lecture, I allude for a moment or two to the loss the University has sustained in the death of its munificent benefactor, Sir Cowasjee Jehanghier. By these and many other acts of munificence Sir Cowasjee has won a place for himself in the roll of public benefactors—out of whom we of this University are chiefly bound to remember Sir Cowasjee and Mr. Premchund Roychund—of whom this great city is so justly proud, and the departed among whom it holds in grateful remembrance." Public respect and sympathy were shown by the closing of the banks, the Parsee shops, the schools, Elphinstone College, and the Share Bazaar.

The funeral ceremony took place at the family

READYMONEY HOUSE,
MALABAR HILL, BOMBAY.

residence on Malabar Hill, and nearly the whole of the Parsee community, including all its chief members and the whole body of priesthood were not only present at the ceremony but followed the funeral cortege. Besides the members of his own community, there were also present the principal representatives of the European community. After the religious ceremonies at Malabar Hill were concluded, a procession was formed and headed by Sir Frank Souter, the then Commissioner of Police of Bombay, proceeded to Chowpati, where, as a descendant of the Dadv Sett family his remains were deposited in the Tower of Silence, belonging to that family. After the usual prayers large sums of money were distributed among the poor, the lame, the blind, and the priests, of whom there were not fewer than 1,500 on the ground. At the third day's funeral obsequies similar ceremonies were scrupulously observed, and further distributions of largesse were made to the poor, by Mr. Jehanghier, as the heir of the deceased knight. In short, nothing was left undone to make the ceremony as imposing and impressive as possible, and the funeral of Sir Cowasjee was long referred to as one of the most magnificent functions in the history of modern Bombay. With every mark of respect on the part of the Bombay community, European, Hindu, and Mahomedan, as well as Parsee, was carried to his last resting-place the most worthy Sir Cowasjee Jehanghier Readymoney, and not only with respect, but with the liveliest feelings of affection which he had aroused by so many acts of private as well as public generosity. Some short time after the funeral, the Parsee Punchayat, or communal assembly, called a special public meeting of the whole Parsee community, and passed a vote of condolence with Sir Cowasjee's family on the irreparable loss they and the city of Bombay had alike suffered. They also addressed a letter of regret to the mother, the heir, and other relatives of the deceased. This, it may be stated, is the greatest possible honour that can be paid to a Parsee, and has rarely been accorded. One final incident in Sir Cowasjee's career may be mentioned, especially as it was not in accordance with Parsee practice, and showed rather the influence. English customs had acquired over his mind. He left by his will annuities and legacies to all his personal servants.

List of public Charities made by Sir Cowasjee Jehangbier, Kt.

			RUPEES.
1846	...	Dr. Bremner's Dispensary, called now Native General Dispensary	1,000
1850	...	For erecting 37 huts, tiled roofs, for sufferers by fire at Camatepoora	1,225
,,	...	District Benevolent Society	1,000
1852	...	Bombay Association	500
,,	...	Perry Testimonial Fund	1,000
1853	...	Prize Money, School of Industry	1,026
1854	...	Bandora Dispensary...	500
,,		Sir J. J. Benevolent Institution	...
1858	...	Scottish Female Orphanage and Poonah Orphanage, for Building and Clothing	5,971
1859	...	Victoria Museum	2.600
1861	...	North-Western Famine Fund	10,000
1861 1862 }	...	Cowasjee Jehanghier *Civil Hospital*, Surat	71,902
1862	...	Manchester Distress Fund	1,000
,,	...	Lancashire Relief Fund	2,000
1863	...	Sir Cowasjee Jehanghier *University Hall* ...	100,000
,,	...	Poonah *Engineering College*	50,000
1863	...	Strangers' Home Friend Society	50,000
,,	...	Royal Asiatic Society for Oriental Work	5,000
,,	...	University *Seal*	1,200
,,	...	Pajrapore Fund, Porebunder	2,200
,,	...	Alexandra Girls' School Fund	5,000

1863 ...	Tower, St. John's Church, Colaba	7,500
1864 ...	Royal Asiatic Society for purchasing Coins	8,000
„ ...	Distressed Weavers, Madras	5,000
„ ...	Elphinstone College, for Sanskrit Books	1,000
„ ...	Calcutta Relief Fund	5,000
1865 ...	Sailors' Home, Bombay	1,500
„ ...	Albert Orphanage Asylum in London	4,752
1866 ...	Cowasjee Jehanghier Eye Hospital	112,000
„ ...	Cowasjee Jehanghier, Building of Elphinstone College...	200,000
„ ...	Fountain, St. Thomas's Cathedral, Bombay	13,777
„ ...	Cowasjee Jehanghier Nowsaree Madrasa, 5 per cent. Government Notes	1,100
1867 ...	Tower at Kapurwange and Library at Kaira Collectorate	2,500
„ ...	Financial Association of India and China...	200,000
„ ...	Charges incurred in maintaining the following Dispensaries :	

~~ Dispensary, from 1862-71~~~	...	Rs.	12,500
Gundevee	„	„	1865-68	... „	5,500
Nowsaree	„	„	1864-67	... „	4,565
Bulsar	„	„	1862-71	... „	11,500

$$34,065$$

1867 ...	Charges incurred in maintaining the following Schools :	
	Gundevee School, from 1864-69 ... ... Rs. 14,000	
	Khetwady Girls' School, from 1859-70 ... „ 22,500	
	Cowasjee Jehanghier Nowsaree Madrasa ... „ 35,000	

$$71,500$$

1867 ...	Cost of Drinking Fountains and their erection in different streets of Bombay, Rs. 30,000 ; Parsee Punchayat Subscription Lame and Blind Fund ; Small amounts in different Associations, Libraries, and Dispensaries	210,288
1867 ...	Nowsaree Madrasa in 5 per cent. Government Notes ...	529
1868 ...	Parsee Punchayat Lame and Blind Fund	500
„ ...	Parsee Punchayat Carrying Dead Body Fund	585

1868	...	Latin Scholarship, Bombay University	5,000
„	...	Grant Medical College, for purchasing Works on Natural History	2,000
„	...	Bombay Association	1,000
„	...	London Printers' Pension Association, London	1,046
„	...	Parsee Punchayat Oriental Languages Teaching Fund	5,000
„	...	Native General Library	1,100
„	...	Lunatic Asylum and Garden in Scinde, Hydrabad ...	50,000
1869	...	Erection of Fountain, Regent's Park, London	13,544
„	...	Grant Medical College, for two Scholarships	5,514
„	...	Indian Turf Society... ...·	5,400
„	...	Irani Fund for supplying Dinners to Indigent Poor ...	3,815
„	...	East India Association in London	1,112
„	...	Female Normal School, for Scholarship	1,500
„	...	Tower, St. Zavier College, Bombay	5,000
„	...	Latin Scholarship, St. Zavier College	2,742
„	...	Scholarship, Grant Medical College	4,130
„	...	Cowasjee Jehanghier Nowsaree Madrasa	1,080
„	...	Subscriptions to different Charitable Institutions in London	2,000
„	...	Duke of Edinburgh's Reception Fund	2,000
„	...	Echapore Parsee Dead Body Carrying Fund	1,080
1870	...	Cowasjee Jehanghier Gundevee English School... ...	3,000
„	...	Indian Medical Department for Experimental Vaccination	540
„	...	Kandawalla Mohla Reading Room and Library, 4 per cent. Government Notes	500
„	...	Cowasjee Jehanghier Gundevee School and Dispensary, 4 per cent. Government Notes	1,000
„	...	Franco-Prussian War, Soldiers' Distressed Fund ...	10,726
1871	...	Cowasjee Jehanghier Khetwady Girls' School	1,000
„	...	The Parsee Zujia Fund for the Relief of Destitute Parsees in Persia	9,975
„	...	Famine Fund for Destitute Parsees in Persia	1,000

1871	...	Echapore General Fund, 4 per cent. Government Notes	500
,,	...	Cowasjee Jehanghier Gundevee Charitable School and Dispensary	500
,,	...	Bombay Philharmonic Society	500
,,	...	Famine Fund for Destitute Parsees in Persia	501
,,		For erection of Dhuramsala (Rest House) at Chowpatty, in Bombay, for Distressed Parsees who come out from Persia	15,000
,,	...	Distribution of £200 in London in commemoration of the Prince of Wales' recovery from serious illness ...	2,048
1872	...	Dr. Livingstone Search Fund, through Sir G. Birdwood	1,026
,,	...	Flying Squadron Sailors' Entertainment Fund	1,000
,,	...	Lord "Northbrook Prize," Alexandra Girls' School ...	500
,,	...	Sir Seymore Fitzgerald Memorial Fund	500
,,	...	Rustomjee Jamsetjee Jeejeebhoy Memorial Fund ...	1,400
,,	...	Protestant Institution	2,000
,,		,, ,, ,, ,, ,, ...	.,...
,,	...	Dadabhoy Nowrosejee Testimonial Fund	500
,,	...	Catholic Christian Institution	1,000
,,	..	Nowsaree Madrasa, 4 per cent. Government Notes ...	500
,,	...	Khandesh and Nassick Relief Fund, in honour of Lord Northbrook's Visit to India	1,000
1873	...	Publication "Shakespeare's Play Fund" in London ...	1,052
1874	...	Bengal Relief Fund...	1,000
,,	...	Furniture for Cowasjee Jehanghier University Hall, to Government of Bombay	10,000
,,	...	John Connon Memorial Fund	1,000
1875	...	Grant Medical College, Midwifery Class	2,045
,,	...	Cowasjee Jehanghier Nowsaree Madrasa	1,200
,,	...	O'Brien Family Fund	1,000
,,	...	Fort Reading Room and Library	1,000
,,	...	Donation to Bhuleshwar Library	500

1875	...	Donation to European Gymkhana in Bombay ...	...			500
,,	...	For Mahim Garden, to Bombay Municipality	...		...	2,500
,,	...	Ahmedabad Relief Fund ...	...	...	...	1,500
,,	...	Tower of Silence Fund, Parsee Punchayat		...	...	1,000
,,	...	Ellis Prize, School of Art, Bombay	...	...	...	1,034
,,	...	Royal Portsmouth Sailors' Home...	...	...	...	556
,,	...	Prince of Wales' Reception Fund...	...	...		2,000
1876	...	Cowasjee Jehanghier Nowsaree Madrasa ...	...	...	...	1,200
,,	...	For Furniture, European Gymkhana in Bombay			...	1,000
,,	...	Reservoirs with Fountains and Drinking Trough at Penn				3,000
,,	...	For repairing Parsee Fire Temple at Gowalia, Tank			...	3,000
,,	...	Nowsaree Madrasa ...	...	...	...	1,200
,,	...	Southern Maharata Famine Relief Fund...		...	...	2,000
,,	...	Bandora Charitable Dispensary, in Government Notes...				10,000
,,	...	For Corporation Seal, to Bombay Municipality ...			..	2,196
,,	...	Sir Jamsetjee Jeejeebhoy, Second Baronet, Memorial Fund ...	...	...	...	1,500
,,	...	Elphinstone College, for purchasing Scientific Books	...			500
		TOTAL	...	...	Rs.	1,442,706

Sir Cowasjee's Private Charities come to about Rs. 300,000

An English friend of mine, who occupied an important position in Bombay many years and was well acquainted with most of the public men of the period, hands me the following notes on some of the characteristics of Sir Cowasjee Jehanghier, which may be of interest :—

"Though all the world knows of the munificence and well-directed benevolence of Sir Cowasjee, his shrewdness and good sense in commercial affairs is not so generally appreciated by the present generation. This may be partly because of his having been withdrawn, by reason of his physical infirmity, from active life so early, though his mental faculties remained as clear as ever. He used to take a prominent part in the proceedings of the Bench of Justices—then the Corporation of Bombay, and I have traced his name in the records of that body. He was, for instance, one of those who, after many investigations, joined in the protest of the Justices against what they regarded as the unduly onerous terms imposed by the Local Government on the city in respect of the debt incurred in the construction of the Vehar Water Works—a burden which still pursues the present Corporation. Sir Cowasjee was, in its best days, on the Board of the Bank of Bombay ; and I have always considered that if he had not been prevented by his illness from continuing his services in that capacity, he might have done much towards saving that institution from the errors in its management which contributed to stimulate, instead of checking the tide of speculation in which the Bank itself was finally overturned with such disastrous effects to many innocent victims. His shrewdness and foresight were just those qualities that were so urgently needed from 1863 to 1865, when the Directors, with so many others, lost their heads amidst the excitement that prevailed.

When in 1861 Mr. James Wilson's heavy income tax was imposed as one of the stringent measures required to restore the Indian finances after the vast expenditure caused by the Mutiny, Sir Cowasjee was one of the mercantile citizens of Bombay who were requested by Government to sit as Assessors and Commissioners for the management of that new levy. Sir Bartle Frere, the Honourable Mr. Gibbs, and other Civilians of the period have often testified to the value of your predecessor's services in that public duty. In 1869, when the heavy expenditure under the Corporation had brought its finances into difficulties and much alarm prevailed, Sir Cowasjee did his part towards reassuring the public mind by making an offer—conditional, I believe, on other citizens coming forward—to advance funds towards paying the more pressing claims. Though this affords a good example of his enlightened public spirit, the mischief had then gone too far for such voluntary aid to be effectual, and new taxation had to be devised to fill up the deficiency.

One of the methods adopted to replenish the municipal coffers was the re-imposition of an octroi or town duties. On a friend of mine (who was then or just afterwards Secretary of the Chamber of Commerce) explaining this to Sir Cowasjee, he exclaimed, "Why, that's Peishwa system!" He found it difficult to understand how any British authorities could consent to adopt the old Native State custom of levying tolls on trade and food.

He was generally, if not always, on the side of the latest improvements in administration, and cherished some of the popular prejudices against the old Company and the Civilians brought up under its régime. An illustration of this occurs to me, which amused the Bombay public at the time. The judges of the High Court comprise Civilian as well as "barrister" judges; but the Chief Justice is generally selected from the latter, the class of English trained lawyers; though there is not, I believe, any statutory regulation to that effect. On one occasion, during the absence of the Chief Justice (the late Sir Michael Westropp), a Civilian judge, the Honourable Henry Newton, was appointed to act for him. Sir Cowasjee at once wrote to the chief daily paper, protesting most energetically against what he regarded as an innovation. His language on this matter was no less quaint than forcible, being the natural outcome of his strong convictions of the advantage of a Chief Justice being one who, having passed through the forensic conflicts of the Bar, would be enabled to hold his own against "bombarding barristers," as Sir Cowasjee styled them. He cited as one example of these champions of the rights of the subject, Mr. Reginald Branson, who, in the trial of an employé of the Bank of Bombay charged with misuse of the Bank's funds, had succeeded in "getting his man off." This trial being in the District Court at Poonah, was necessarily before a Civilian judge; hence the incident served as an illustration of the argument in the letter which impugned the discretion, and almost the right, of the Local Government to place a Civilian judge at the head of the High Court. However, Mr. Justice Newton, who was a sound lawyer and a very estimable man, only held the position for a few months; and I believe Sir Cowasjee considered that his prompt protest had some effect, for the innovation has not since been repeated.

Sir Cowasjee Jehanghier very highly prized the distinction of the title bestowed on. him, though it is no secret that he hoped to have lived to receive the hereditary distinction of a baronetcy. On receiving the honour of knighthood, he wrote in reply to my felicitations:—

As Sir Cowasjee's notes lie before me in his easy, flowing handwriting —which are indeed interspersed with pathetic references to his often acute sufferings—it has been a pleasure, not untinged with melancholy, as I recall the many interesting experiences I had with him both in his old house in the Fort and in his residence on Lower Malabar Hill. It may be well to add a passage from the note I had from his brother Heerjee, in response to my expression of regret at the loss his family and the city had suffered in Sir Cowasjee's decease :—

"You have rightly estimated his high character and intelligence, but this is not the time for me to say much about it here, beyond remarking that all those who had the occasion to come into contact with him had invariably formed the high opinion of him that you have now so kindly expressed."

www.ingramcontent.com/pod-product-compliance
Lightning Source LLC
Chambersburg PA
CBHW022015050726
47499CB00007BA/2659